Unicorn Princesses

BREEZE'S BLAST

Unicorn Princesses

BREEZE'S BLAST

Emily Bliss

illustrated by Sydney Hanson

BLOOMSBURY

NEW YORK LONDON OXFORD NEW DELHI SYDNEY

First published in the United States of America in April 2018
by Bloomsbury Children's Books
www.bloomsbury.com

Bloomsbury is a registered trademark of Bloomsbury Publishing Plc

For information about permission to reproduce selections from this book, write to
Permissions, Bloomsbury Children's Books, 1385 Broadway, New York, NY 10018
Bloomsbury books may be purchased for business or promotional use.
For information on bulk purchases please contact Macmillan Corporate and
Premium Sales Department at specialmarkets@macmillan.com

Library of Congress Cataloging-in-Publication Data
Names: Bliss, Emily, author. | Hanson, Sydney, illustrator.
Title: Breeze's blast / by Emily Bliss ; illustrated by Sydney Hanson.
Description: New York : Bloomsbury, 2018. | Series: Unicorn princesses ; 5
Summary: Princess Breeze invites her human friend, Cressida, to attend the Blast,
a festival featuring kite flying, but the wizard-lizard, Ernest, has blundered again
and now giant bats sleep on the kites.
Identifiers: LCCN 2017020574 (print) | LCCN 2017036915 (e-book)
ISBN 978-1-68119-649-7 (paperback) • ISBN 978-1-68119-650-3 (hardcover)
ISBN 978-1-68119-651-0 (e-book)
Subjects: | CYAC: Festivals—Fiction. | Kites—Fiction. | Bats—Fiction. |
Unicorns—Fiction. | Princesses—Fiction. | Magic—Fiction. | Fantasy.
Classification: LCC PZ7.1.B633 Bre 2018 (print) | LCC PZ7.1.B633 (e-book) |
DDC [Fic]—dc23
LC record available at https://lccn.loc.gov/2017020574

Book design by Jessie Gang and John Candell
Typeset by Westchester Publishing Services
Printed and bound in the U.S.A. by Berryville Graphics Inc., Berryville, Virginia
2 4 6 8 10 9 7 5 3 1 (paperback)
2 4 6 8 10 9 7 5 3 1 (hardcover)

For Phoenix and Lynx

Unicorn Princesses

Princesses

BREEZE'S BLAST

Chapter One

In the top tower of Spiral Palace, Ernest, the wizard-lizard, stared at his bookshelf. He tilted his scaly green head to one side and his pointy hat almost toppled off. "Hmm," he said. "What book of spells should I study next? *Magic Storms and Other Bewitched Weather*? No, the unicorn princesses wouldn't like that much. *Enchanted Bangs and Conjured Crashes*? Nope, too loud. What about—"

Before he could finish his sentence, a loud thumping on the door interrupted him. "Come in!" he called out, straightening his hat and cloak.

The wooden door creaked open, and a red dragon wearing a white chef's hat and apron entered. "Good morning, Ernest!" the dragon boomed. His flame-colored eyes glimmered, and blue smoke puffed from his nostrils. In one clawed hand he held eight bulbs of garlic.

"Hello, Drew," Ernest said, smiling eagerly. "Can I help you with something?"

"You sure can!" Drew bellowed. "We dragons down in the palace kitchen were wondering if you might provide us with some magical assistance."

"With pleasure!" Ernest said, jumping with glee.

"Fantastic," Drew said as threads of smoke rose from his nose. "Could you turn these bulbs of garlic into eight large cooking vats? We're preparing to make the Blast Feast for Princess Breeze, but none of our usual pots are big enough."

"I know just the right book of spells!" Ernest exclaimed. He grabbed a thin red book entitled *Magic in the Kitchen* and flipped to a page that said, in large letters across

the top, "Big Pots, Large Pans, Giant Vats, and Humongous Cauldrons."

"Thank you!" Drew said, and he set the garlic bulbs down on Ernest's table.

"I'm sure I can do this one perfectly on the first try," Ernest said. He read over the spell several times, mouthing the words silently. Then he stepped up to his table, grabbed his magic wand from his cloak pocket, and lifted it into the air. He took a deep breath before he chanted, "Cookily Slookily Stockily Stew! Garlic Starlic Smarlic Smew! Make Eight Bats for a Tasty Brew!"

Ernest waited. The bulbs of garlic didn't spin or jump or quiver. Instead, thunder rumbled. Ernest scratched his head. "Oh dear," Ernest said. "I'm not sure why that didn't work."

"Well," Drew said, "I'm not a wizard, so I don't know for sure, but I think it's because you said 'bats' instead of 'vats.'"

"Oh dear!" Ernest said again, slapping his hand to his forehead. Ernest turned and looked out the window just as eight bolts of silver lightning tore through the sky right above a distant meadow.

Drew shrugged. "We all make mistakes," he said. "I usually have to try a recipe five or six times before I get it right."

"Hopefully Princess Breeze won't notice anything is amiss before the Blast," Ernest said. Then he turned toward the garlic, cleared his throat, lifted his wand, and chanted, "Cookily Slookily Stockily Stew! Garlic Starlic Smarlic Smew! Make Eight Vats for a Tasty Brew!"

The bulbs of garlic spun around, faster and faster. Then, with a swirl of wind and a bright flash of light, the garlic vanished, and a tower of eight enormous silver vats appeared by the door.

"Marvelous!" Drew boomed, and a huge cloud of smoke came out of his nose. "I'm impressed you got it on the second try. Well done!"

"Thank you," Ernest said, blushing.

Drew turned to the stack of vats and hoisted two off the top. "These are heavy!

I'll take these down to the kitchen, and then I'll come back and get the rest. Thanks again for your help!" The dragon, with one arm wrapped around each vat, lumbered out of the room.

Chapter Two

Early one Saturday morning, Cressida Jenkins watched the willow trees in her backyard bend and sway in the wind, and she decided to build her first-ever homemade kite.

While her parents drank coffee and talked in the kitchen, Cressida collected sticks, scissors, tape, and markers from her desk drawer. She found a pink plastic bag under the kitchen sink and then sat down with her supplies on the living room floor. Corey, her older brother, lay on the couch drinking orange juice and reading *All About Bats*, a book he had gotten from their grandmother for his birthday.

Cressida cut the plastic bag into a large diamond. She arranged the sticks into a cross and taped them to the diamond. Next, she used the markers to decorate the pink plastic with pictures of the seven unicorn princesses Cressida had befriended: yellow Sunbeam, silver Flash, green Bloom, purple Prism, blue Breeze, black Moon, and orange Firefly.

Corey glanced at Cressida's kite and rolled his eyes. "Are you ever going to stop

being obsessed with unicorns?" he asked. "Bats are much better. For one thing, they're actually real. And, they can fly. Did you know they sleep all day and hunt mosquitoes and other insects all night? I bet unicorns, even if they were real, couldn't do that."

Cressida shrugged. She had much better things to do—like fly her kite—than argue with her brother. "I like unicorns *and* bats," she said as she used a light blue marker to put the final touches on Breeze's mane and tail.

Little did Corey know that not only were unicorns just as real as bats, but that any time she wanted to, Cressida could visit the Rainbow Realm—a magical land ruled by the unicorn princesses. To travel there, all she had to do was push a special key into a secret hole in the base of a giant oak tree in the woods behind their house.

"Why are the unicorns wearing those strange things around their necks?" Corey asked, frowning as he studied her kite.

"They're magic necklaces," Cressida explained. Just like the real princess unicorns, each of the unicorns Cressida had drawn wore a magic gemstone that hung from a colored ribbon.

Corey sighed. "Magic isn't real, either," he said.

Cressida smiled mysteriously. "That's what you think," she replied, not bothering to look up. When her grandmother had visited for Corey's birthday, she'd given Cressida a set of permanent markers in metallic shades. Now, Cressida used the gold one to color in Sunbeam's hooves and horn.

"Things that are real can be pretty amazing," Corey said, looking down at his open book. "Did you know that the biggest kind of bats have a wingspan of up to six feet? Can you imagine a bat that big?"

"That's pretty neat," Cressida said, pausing to imagine a bat with a wingspan that was just as long as her father was tall.

"Maybe I'll make a gigantic bat kite after I finish this book," Corey said.

"I'll help you with it," Cressida said.

Then, as Corey continued to read,

Cressida drew a rainbow that arched over the unicorn princesses.

Now the only thing left to do before she could fly her kite was to make it a tail. Cressida stood up and skipped across the living room, down the hall, and into her bedroom. She pulled her art supply bin off her shelves. And just as she began to rummage through a mess of paints, markers, crayons, yarn, stickers, glue, tape, sequins, and beads, she heard a high, tinkling noise.

Cressida grinned and leaped across the room to her bedside table. She opened the drawer and pulled out an old-fashioned key with a crystal ball handle. The ball glowed bright pink as the key continued to make the tinkling noise. It was the special signal the unicorns used to invite her to visit them in the Rainbow Realm!

Cressida, who was still wearing her green unicorn pajamas, changed into a pair of jeans, a teal T-shirt with a picture of a kite with a rainbow tail, and her favorite shoes: a pair of silver unicorn sneakers. She especially loved them because they had pink lights that blinked whenever she walked, ran, or jumped.

With the key safely stowed in the back pocket of her jeans, Cressida dashed out of her room and sprinted to the back door.

"Where are you going in such a hurry?" Corey called out. "And aren't you going to take your kite?"

"I'll be right back," Cressida said as she

stepped outside. "I'm just going for a quick walk in the woods before I try to fly it."

"Have fun," Cressida's father called from the kitchen.

Fortunately, time in the human world froze while Cressida was in the Rainbow Realm, so even if she spent hours with the unicorns, Corey and her parents would think she'd been gone only a few minutes.

Cressida ran through her backyard and turned onto her favorite path in the woods behind her house. When she came to the giant oak, she kneeled down and found the tiny hole in the base of the tree. Her heart thundered with excitement as she pushed the key into the hole. The forest began to spin, turning into a whirl of brown and green, and then everything turned pitch black. Suddenly Cressida felt as though she were falling through space. Then, with a gentle thud, she landed on something soft. For a moment, all she could see was a blur of white, pink, and purple. But when the room stopped spinning, Cressida found

herself sitting on a lavender armchair in the front hall of Spiral Palace, the unicorns' white, sparkling, horn-shaped home.

Crystal chandeliers shimmered from the ceiling. Light poured in through the windows, as pink, purple, and silver curtains fluttered in the breeze. Cressida looked all around the room for her unicorn friends, but the unicorn-size velvet couches and chairs were empty.

"Hello?" Cressida called out, standing up and walking to the center of the room. "Is anyone here?"

Then she heard a clattering of hooves in the hallway. In a few seconds, all seven unicorn princesses trotted up to Cressida.

Chapter Three

Breeze danced over to Cressida and sang out, "Yippee! You're here! We were trying to sneak into the palace kitchen to see what the dragons are cooking, but they caught us!" Her magic gemstone—an aquamarine—hung from an orange ribbon around her neck and glittered in the light of the chandeliers. From her other trips to the Rainbow Realm,

Cressida knew Breeze's magic power was to create gusts of blue wind.

"My human girl is back!" Sunbeam sang out, clicking her gold hooves together.

"We're so glad you could come," Flash said, swishing her silver tail.

Bloom and Prism reared up with excitement. And Firefly winked at Cressida.

The only unicorn who didn't look happy was Moon, who stood apart from her sisters and stared worriedly at her shiny black hooves.

Cressida wanted to ask Moon what was wrong, but before she could, Breeze gushed, "We invited you here for our annual Windy Meadows Blast. It's my favorite day of the year, and I'm so excited I can't stand still."

Breeze trotted backward in circles around Cressida. "You're just in time to come to the Windy Meadows to help me prepare for the Blast. Will you join me? Please!"

Cressida giggled. "Of course I will," she said. "But what is the Blast?"

"It's a special day when all my sisters and I ride huge kites up into the clouds," Breeze explained. "Afterwards, the dragons cook us a fantastic feast. We want you to be the first human girl to ride up into the clouds with us."

"I'd love that," Cressida said. Flying into the clouds on a kite with seven unicorns sounded like more fun than almost anything else Cressida could imagine doing that morning.

Moon frowned and sighed loudly. Cressida opened her mouth to ask Moon what was wrong, but before she could speak, a red dragon wearing a puffy white hat and apron appeared. He whistled as he carried two enormous metal vats through the palace's front room and down a hallway that led to the kitchen. Cressida knew from her first visit to the Rainbow Realm that the dragons were chefs who cooked the unicorns' food with their fiery breath.

"Won't you please tell us what you're making for the Blast feast?" Breeze called out when she saw the dragon.

The dragon laughed, and blue smoke poured from his nostrils. "No chance!" he chortled. "It's a secret. But you're going to

love it! We've been practicing the recipes
for weeks. Now, if you'll excuse me, I need
to put these vats in the kitchen and go
get the rest of the ones Ernest made for
me." With that, he disappeared down the
hall, his enormous, spiked tale dragging
behind him.

"I'm already hungry for the Blast feast,"
Breeze said. "I skipped breakfast so I'd have
extra room."

"Me too!" Sunbeam and Flash said at
once.

Flash turned to Sunbeam and nar-
rowed her eyes. "*You* did?" she asked. "That
doesn't sound like you."

Sunbeam blushed. "Well, okay, I had
a little bit of breakfast," she admitted.

"I started to get cranky because I was hungry and I ate some roinkleberries. Well, a lot of roinkleberries. And some mushrooms. And an avocado. But trust me, I'm already hungry for the feast!"

"Prism, Firefly, and I meant to just have a small breakfast," Bloom said, smiling self-consciously, "but then we saw a cluster of huge, perfectly ripe froyananas hanging from a tree. And, well, we couldn't resist!"

Cressida's stomach turned. When she had visited Bloom's domain, the Enchanted Garden, she had taken one bite of a froyanana only to discover it tasted like a terrible mix of pickles, marshmallows, tomatoes, and tuna fish.

Prism nodded. "They were amazing!

But by the time the dragons have cooked their feast, I'm sure we'll be hungry."

"Definitely," Firefly added. "I can't wait for all of us to fly up into the sky together."

Moon glanced up, and Cressida could see the unicorn's eyes had filled with tears.

"What's wrong, Moon?" Cressida asked.

Moon sniffled. "I'm not coming to the Blast this year, or ever again," she said. "I'm too scared."

"Oh no," Flash whispered to Cressida. "Moon fell off her kite last year, and although she didn't get hurt, she's been terrified of this year's Blast ever since."

Cressida nodded. She certainly understood what it felt like to be scared after an accident—once, she had fallen off a playground swing, and she hadn't wanted to go anywhere near that swing set, or even that park, afterward. Later, when she felt ready, she had returned to the park with her friends Gillian and Eleanor, and she had even tried—and enjoyed—swinging. But it had taken her awhile to feel like swinging again.

Breeze looked at Moon and said, "I know you're scared, but you have to come to the Blast. It won't be any fun without you."

"I'm sure you won't fall off again this year," Sunbeam said.

Moon shook her head, and more tears streamed down her cheeks.

"Come on, Moon," Prism said. "We all want you to fly with us."

"I told you, I'm not coming," Moon said. "Would you please listen to me? Stop trying to make me do something I don't want to do!" With that, she turned and galloped down the hallway.

Breeze frowned. "I feel bad for Moon, but I just really hope she changes her mind," she said. "The Blast won't be any fun without all of us there, flying together."

"I'll go talk to her as soon as you and Cressida leave for the Windy Meadows to prepare for the Blast," Flash said. "Don't worry! I'm sure I can convince her to come fly with us."

"Thank you, Flash!" Breeze said, and her eyes lit back up with excitement. She turned to Cressida. "Are you ready to come with me to the Windy Meadows? I can't wait to show you around."

"Absolutely!" Cressida said. Though she felt excited to visit the Windy Meadows, she also felt worried about Moon. She hoped the other unicorns would be able to comfort their sister.

"What are we waiting for? Let's go!" Breeze called out, kneeling down. But just as Cressida started to climb onto Breeze's back, a high, nasal voice cried, "Hold on! Wait!" And then Cressida heard the unmistakable sound of Ernest, the wizard-lizard, running as fast as his feet could carry him down the hall and toward the front room of the palace.

"Hello, Ernest!" Cressida said, giggling.

"Before you go," Ernest said, "I have a present for you! I've been practicing this spell for the past hour, and I'm absolutely sure I've finally gotten it right!"

Cressida smiled and braced herself for a magical mishap. Every time she came to the Rainbow Realm, Ernest got at least one spell wrong.

The wizard-lizard took a deep breath. He pulled his wand from his cloak. And then he chanted, "Safety Sequiny Satiny Bright! Make a Magic Grape for Cressida's Flight!"

A gust of wind swirled around Cressida.

And then she felt something cool, wet, and mushy against her skin. She looked down and laughed to see that she was inside a giant, bright blue, sequin-covered grape. Only her head stuck out from the top.

"Oh dear!" Ernest exclaimed.

The giant grape, with Cressida inside it, began to roll forward. "Yikes!" Cressida said as Breeze and Bloom rushed over and used their hooves to keep her upright.

"Oops," Ernest said. "When I was practicing upstairs, I kept accidentally making apes. And one time I even made a roll of tape. But a grape is something new. Hold on. Oh dear!"

Ernest scratched his head. He raised his wand. And he chanted, "Gibbledy Globbledy Gobbledy Goo! Trade in this Grape for a Cape of Blue!"

More wind swirled around Cressida, and, to her relief, the giant grape vanished and now both her feet were firmly planted on the ground. When she looked down, she saw she was wearing a long, bright turquoise, sequined cape.

"Wow! I love it!" Cressida said, twirling around so the cape billowed.

Ernest grinned with delight. "It's a special magic cape," he explained. "If you fall off your kite, it will keep you from getting hurt when you land on the ground. It came out just a little larger than I expected. I hope you don't mind."

"It's absolutely perfect. Thank you, Ernest," Cressida said. Then she looked at Breeze. "How do I look?" she asked.

"Ready to fly!" Breeze exclaimed.

Cressida looked at her reflection on the marble floor and smiled: she thought she looked just like a superhero. She made a fist and extended her hand up into the air, as though she were about to fly up into the sky.

"What are you doing?" asked Flash.

"I'm pretending to be a superhero!" Cressida said.

"A superhero?" Breeze asked. "What's that?"

"Well," Cressida said, "a superhero is a human with magic powers who solves problems. They aren't real, but it's fun to pretend to be one."

"Huh," Breeze and Sunbeam said at the same time.

Then Breeze shrugged and said, "Let's go!" She kneeled down, and Cressida climbed onto her back.

Breeze turned toward the other unicorn princesses and said, "We'll see you in the Windy Meadows. Make sure you bring Moon!" And with Cressida on her back she raced out the palace's front door.

Chapter Four

C ressida gripped Breeze's silky, light blue mane as the unicorn raced along the path of clear stones that led away from Spiral Palace and into the surrounding forest. Cressida turned, and for a few seconds she watched the tall, glittering white palace, shaped like a unicorn horn, fade into the distance.

"The only thing we really need to do to

get ready for the Blast is to make sure the kites are lined up and ready to fly," Breeze said, jumping playfully as she galloped. "That means we have time for me to show you my two very favorite parts of the Windy Meadows first."

"What are they?" Cressida asked, feeling her heart beat with excitement.

"It's a surprise!" Breeze sang out as she turned down a narrow path that cut through a thicket of pine trees.

"I can't wait," Cressida said, grinning. She loved surprises, and the Rainbow Realm was always full of surprises that were even better than anything she could imagine.

Breeze followed the path across a patch of blue mushrooms, up a fern-covered hill, and over to a grove of willow trees.

"We're almost there!" Breeze said. "Close your eyes!"

Cressida squeezed her eyes shut as Breeze turned sharply to the right, slowed down, and stopped. "Okay! You can look now," the unicorn said.

When Cressida opened her eyes, she saw that she and Breeze were standing right in the middle of a meadow so full of large orange ball-shaped flowers that she could hardly see any grass.

"Welcome to the Windy Meadows!" Breeze said, kneeling down as Cressida slid off her back. "This meadow is just our first stop. It's called the Meadow of Metamorflowers."

"Are these metamorflowers?" Cressida asked, looking more closely at the flowers. As they brushed against Cressida's knees and the bottom of her cape, she noticed each orange ball was made of what looked like hundreds of tiny feather-shaped petals.

"Not only are they metamorflowers," Breeze said, shuffling her hooves with excitement, "but they're *magic* metamorflowers. I'll show you!"

The unicorn pointed her blue horn toward the sky. The aquamarine on her ribbon necklace shimmered. Glittery light

shot from her horn. And then a blue, comet-shaped gust of wind appeared. First, it bolted straight up into the air and did three somersaults. Then it plunged down to the flowers, where it circled Breeze and Cressida, faster and faster, until Cressida felt as though she were in the center of a small tornado. Thousands of orange petals lifted off the flowers' stems and into the air, and soon Cressida felt as though she were standing in an orange blizzard.

Then the petals fluttered into a large pile right in front of Cressida's feet and Breeze's hooves. Cressida reached down and grabbed a handful of petals. To her surprise, they stuck together, almost like clay or snow.

"Now watch this!" Breeze said, and she used her hooves to roll a clump of petals into what looked like a snake. Then, with her nose, she tossed it upward. To Cressida's amazement, in the air, it transformed into what looked like a real orange snake, slithering above them.

"Yikes!" Cressida said, jumping backward.

"Don't worry," Breeze said, laughing. "It can't hurt you!"

As Cressida watched, fascinated and a little scared, the snake wiggled, slid, and hissed. And then, as suddenly as it had seemed to come alive, the snake turned back to a shower of petals that fluttered to the ground.

"My sisters and I can spend hours here at a time," Breeze said. "The only problem is that since my sisters and I have hooves, the only things we can do are roll and flatten the petals. Since there aren't very many animals that look like pancakes, we end up making a lot of snakes, eels, and worms. And once I even managed a caterpillar." Breeze's eyes filled with excitement. "But I bet, since you have fingers and a thumb, you could make all kinds of animals. Try it!"

Cressida picked up two handfuls of petals and smushed them together. Then, she shaped the petals into a rabbit with long ears, large paws, and a small, fluffy-looking tail.

"Throw it into the air!" Breeze said, bounding from side to side.

Cressida tossed it up, and the rabbit seemed to come alive, hopping, sniffing, and scratching its ears.

Then, right in the middle of a jump, it

fell apart, and the petals fluttered to the ground.

"Wow!" Cressida said, laughing with delight as she grabbed more petals and sculpted a cheetah. "This is much more fun than regular modeling clay!" After she used her fingernail to give the cat's body spots, she launched it into the air and watched as it sprinted in circles over her head.

"That cheetah is an even faster runner than Flash," Breeze said with wide eyes. Flash's magic power was to run so fast that lightning bolts crackled from her horn and hooves.

After the cheetah turned into a shower of petals, Cressida made an eagle that soared and swooped, an elephant that swung its trunk, a monkey that hung from its tail, and an alligator that snapped its jaws as it crept forward. Breeze rolled out five more snakes, three eels, and two earthworms.

"Guess what? I have an idea for an animal we could make together," Cressida said.

"What is it?" Breeze asked, her eyes lighting up.

"It's a surprise," Cressida said, winking. "But if you make eight snakes, I'll make the rest."

As Breeze got to work rolling clumps of petals, Cressida used her hands to sculpt an elongated ball with eyes and a mouth.

Then she attached Breeze's snakes to the ball.

"An octopus!" Breeze exclaimed. "What a great idea!"

Cressida giggled and threw the octopus into the air. It glided above them, waving its tentacles as though it were underwater. And then it fell apart.

Just as Cressida was about to suggest they make a giant spider together in the same way, Breeze sighed and said, "This has been so much fun, but I think we'd better stop and tidy up. I want to make sure there's time to show you one more thing before we check on the kites."

"Of course," Cressida said, feeling both disappointed to leave and curious about what else Breeze wanted to show her. "How can I help tidy up?"

"Thanks so much for offering," Breeze said, "but I always just use magic to clean up the petals. Watch this!" She pointed her horn toward the sky. The aquamarine on her ribbon shimmered as glittery light shot from her horn. A gust of blue wind swirled around Cressida and Breeze. And the petals lifted into the air and returned to their stems, re-forming into the ball-shaped flowers Cressida had seen when they first arrived at the meadow. A gentle breeze riffled through the flowers, and once again they brushed against her knees and the bottom of her cape.

"Wow! That's the quickest cleaning job

I've ever seen," Cressida said, wishing she could use magic to clean her room.

Breeze kneeled down. "Climb on up," she said. "Our next stop is the Meadow of Melodies."

Chapter Five

With Cressida on her back, Breeze trotted under a canopy of green leafy elms and into another meadow, this one dotted with trees and shrubs. A gentle breeze blew, and Cressida heard faint, high-pitched music that reminded her of the sound her key to the Rainbow Realm made when the unicorns invited her to visit. Cressida looked at the

trees and shrubs more carefully and saw that wind chimes hung from nearly every branch. Some were metal and some were wood. The large wind chimes played lower notes, while the small ones played high-pitched music.

Breeze kneeled, and Cressida slid to the ground.

"What song would you like to hear?" Breeze asked, grinning excitedly.

"Hmm," Cressida said, trying to think of a song Breeze might know.

But before she could answer, Breeze said, "How about 'Twinkle, Twinkle, Little Star'?"

Cressida smiled. When she was younger,

that had been one of her favorite songs. "Sure!" she said.

"I have to admit, it's my favorite song," Breeze said, blushing. Then she pointed her horn to the sky. Her aquamarine shimmered. Glittery light shot from her horn, and a star-shaped gust of blue wind appeared, this one smaller and gentler than the one that had appeared in the Meadow of Metamorflowers. The gust danced through the trees and shrubs, and as the branches swayed, Cressida heard the most beautiful rendition of "Twinkle, Twinkle, Little Star" she could have imagined. No wonder it was Breeze's favorite song, she thought. Cressida smiled with delight as the wind chimes played the song over and over, each time a little more faintly, as the gust lost its strength.

"That's really neat," Cressida said.

"I know!" Breeze said. "And now, I think we'd really better go make sure the kites are ready. When I fed them breakfast this morning, they promised they would be all lined up by now. But sometimes they get distracted by an especially good gust of wind, and they're late."

"Wait a minute," Cressida said, smiling with delight. "The kites are alive?" She wasn't sure why she was so surprised. After all, on other visits to the Rainbow Realm, she had met boulders and dunes that talked. And yet, the idea of a talking, laughing, live kite especially delighted her.

"Of course they're alive," said Breeze. "And not only are they alive, but they're a little bit mischievous and wild. They love to fly upside down and in circles in the air. That's why Moon fell off during last year's Blast. Her kite, Kevin, was in an especially rambunctious mood, and he tried to fly too fast." Cressida nodded. Worry flashed across Breeze's face. "I sure do hope Flash has convinced Moon to participate in the Blast by now. Anyway," the unicorn said, her face brightening, "come this way! The kites always line up in the Monarch Meadow."

"The Monarch Meadow?" Cressida asked as they walked along a row of windmills. "Like the butterfly?" In school, they

had learned the names of different butterflies, including monarchs, which were
orange with black markings.

"Exactly!" Breeze said, looking
impressed.

Cressida followed Breeze down a hill,
through a cluster of willow trees, and into
a meadow teeming with wildflowers and
orange-and-black butterflies. In the middle
of all the butterflies and wildflowers were
eight of the biggest, bluest kites she had
ever seen. And on top of each one slept a
silver, furry animal that was twice the size
of a unicorn. Each animal had shiny,
folded wings and large, round ears.

"What are those?" Breeze asked, fur-
rowing her brow.

"Are they giant flying mice?" Cressida asked, walking toward one. When she looked more closely, she saw two sharp teeth poking out from the animal's mouth. "I think they're huge bats," Cressida said. She remembered that Corey had told her that very morning that bats sleep all day and search for food at night. "They must be sleeping because it's daytime."

"Huge bats?" Breeze said, looking pan-icked. "Where did those come from?"

But before Cressida could suggest that one of Ernest's accidental spells might be to blame, a kite called out, "Is that you, Princess Breeze?"

Another said, "Help! We can't get up!"

"Plus, it's awfully hot under here," a third voice added.

"It's me!" called out Breeze. "What happened?"

"Well," one of the kites said, "we had just finished practicing some of our stunts and tricks. And then we were lining up for the Blast when, all of a sudden, lightning flashed. There was an even stronger gust of wind than usual, and the next thing we knew, there was a giant bat sleeping on each of us."

"How will we get them off?" Breeze asked Cressida.

"Well," Cressida said, "Maybe we should start by just asking them to leave."

"Will you do it?" Breeze asked, looking nervous. "I've always been a little afraid of bats. And these are the biggest bats I've ever seen."

"Sure," Cressida said. She walked closer to the bats. "Excuse me," she said. The bats didn't even stir. "Excuse me!" she called out again, this time much louder. The bats blinked and yawned. "I'm sorry to wake you, but I'm wondering if you might sleep somewhere else. Princess Breeze needs these kites."

The bat closest to Cressida frowned. "The trouble," the bat squeaked, "is that it is daytime and we are all very sleepy."

"I don't think," another bat squeaked, "that there is any way that we can get up right now. You'll have to wait until it's nighttime."

"Sorry!" a third bat squeaked.

And with that, all eight bats yawned, closed their eyes, and began to snore.

"Oh no," Breeze said. "Could you possibly try pushing them off the kites?" Cressida looked again at the bats. "I think they're probably too heavy," she said.

Breeze looked as though she might start crying. "Would you be willing to try, just in case it works?" Breeze asked. "I don't know what I'll do if we have to cancel the Blast. All the dragons' hard work cooking our feast would go to waste."

"Okay," Cressida said. "It won't hurt to try!" She walked up to the smallest bat, took a deep breath, and used both hands to push as hard as she could on his back. The bat's fur felt soft against her hands, like a rabbit's. As Cressida shoved with all her might, the bat didn't even stir or open his eyes, let alone move. It would have been easier, she thought, to push a car.

She dropped her arms and walked back to Breeze. "I'm sorry, but they're just too heavy," Cressida said. "But I have another idea. What if you created a gust of wind strong enough to blow them off the kites?"

Breeze smiled hopefully. "Good idea! I'll try it!" she said. Glittery light shot from her horn just before a giant, comet-shaped gust of wind appeared. It bolted over to the bats, blowing hard against their heads, their bodies, and their folded wings. Some of the bats grunted and stretched. But they still didn't wake up, let alone roll off the kites.

"Oh no!" Breeze said, as the wind died down. "That was my very strongest gust of wind ever." The unicorn's top lip quivered. "What if we have to cancel the Blast?" Breeze asked as a tear rolled down her cheek.

Cressida turned, put her arms around Breeze, and said, "There must be a way to get the bats off the kites before the Blast. Let me just think for a moment."

And then Cressida had an idea. She jumped up and down with excitement. "I think I know what to do! But we're going to need to get Moon to help us."

"Let's go back to the palace and get her," Breeze said. "I'll bet Flash and my other sisters have convinced her to fly in the Blast by now!" The unicorn kneeled down, and Cressida climbed onto her back. As soon as Cressida had tightly gripped her mane, Breeze galloped back through the Windy Meadows toward Spiral Palace.

Chapter Six

With Cressida on her back, Breeze sped across the clear stones leading up to the front door of Spiral Palace. When they entered the front room, they found Sunbeam, Flash, Bloom, Prism, Moon, and Firefly standing in a circle.

"I'm not going," Moon said, shaking her head. "Last time was just too scary.

I never want to go anywhere near a giant kite again."

"What if we made sure to give you the calmest kite this year?" Sunbeam asked.

Moon shook her head.

"Would it help if I rode right next to you?" Flash asked.

Moon shook her head again.

"If you want, you could share a kite with me," Prism said. "Would that work?"

"No, but thank you for offering," Moon said.

"But if you don't fly with us, it will ruin the Blast," Bloom said. "It won't be any fun without you."

Moon began to cry, and she stomped

her front hooves angrily. "How many times do I have to tell you? I'm too scared. I'm not flying this year. Please stop trying to make me change my mind."

Breeze loudly cleared her throat, and her six sisters turned toward her. "We weren't expecting to see you back here right before the Blast," Flash said. "Is something wrong?"

"Yes," Breeze said. "When we got to the Windy Meadows, we discovered gigantic bats sleeping on the kites. Cressida tried to shove them off. And I tried to push them off with a gust of wind. But they were too big and heavy. I'm worried we'll have to cancel the Blast."

"There are *bats* on all the kites?" Moon asked, suddenly grinning. She looked absolutely delighted that the Blast might be canceled. Meanwhile, all the other unicorns' faces fell.

"Oh no!" Bloom and Prism said in unison.

"That's terrible," Firefly said.

"Sounds like Ernest made another mistake," Flash said, grimacing.

"What will we do?" Sunbeam asked.

"Well," Breeze said, "Cressida says she has one last idea."

All the unicorn princesses turned toward Cressida. She smiled and nodded. And then she said, "I do have a plan, but we'll need Moon's help."

Moon shook her head. "I'm sorry, but I have to admit I really want the Blast to be canceled. I still have bad dreams about the time I fell off my kite. I don't think I can help you."

Flash, Sunbeam, Bloom, Prism, Firefly, and Breeze all began to talk at once, trying to convince Moon to change her mind.

"Excuse me," Cressida said, politely but loudly. The unicorns stopped talking and turned toward her. Cressida remembered again how scared she had felt of swinging after she had fallen off her swing—and how much she wouldn't have liked anyone pushing her to swing again before she felt ready.

"Moon," Cressida said, "would you be

willing to help get the bats off the kites if your sisters agreed to stop trying to get you to fly in the Blast? Maybe you could just watch this year. Or, if that's too much, you could come back to stay in the palace during the Blast."

Moon thought for a moment, and then she nodded. "I know how much the Blast means to Breeze and my other sisters. If everyone would just stop putting pressure on me to fly, I'd help get the bats off the kites in any way I can." She looked at Breeze and continued, "I don't actually want you to have to cancel the Blast. It's just that I feel much too scared to ride a kite this year. And I don't like all of you

trying to convince me to do something
I really don't want to do."

"That makes perfect sense to me," Cressida said to Moon, smiling reassuringly.
Then she looked at the other unicorns. "I
know all of you really want Moon to fly
with you in the Blast, but she's saying she's

not ready and it won't be fun for her. If she agrees to help get the bats off the kites, will you agree to stop trying to get her to fly?"

"Yes," Breeze said. "I'll be sad if Moon doesn't fly with us. But I don't want to cancel the Blast." She paused and thought for a moment. And then she looked at Moon. "I really do understand that you're just not ready to fly this year." The other unicorns nodded in agreement. "And I'm sorry we all kept trying to convince you to fly with us," Breeze continued. "I just always think things are more fun when we're all together. But Cressida is right. I should have listened when you said you were too scared."

"I forgive you," Moon said, grinning at

her sister. "Now let's go get those bats off the kites before it's too late!"

"Great," said Cressida. "If Breeze, Moon, and I go back to the Windy Meadows now, I think we'll be able to get the bats off the kites in time to hold the Blast."

Breeze kneeled down so Cressida could climb on her back, and, with Moon following right behind them, Breeze galloped out the front door. "See you very soon!" Breeze called.

Chapter Seven

"The first thing we need to do," Cressida said as she rode Breeze through the forest toward the Windy Meadows, "is pay another visit to the metamorflowers."

"Oh, I love the metamorflowers!" gushed Moon, who was galloping alongside Breeze. "My specialty is making extra-long earthworms!" Moon grinned, and Cressida felt relieved that the unicorn now seemed much happier.

"Cressida and I made an octopus together," Breeze said.

"It must be pretty neat to have fingers and thumbs," Moon said.

"It must be pretty neat to have magic powers," Cressida responded.

The three of them laughed.

Soon, Breeze, Moon, and Cressida stood in the center of the Meadow of Metamor-flowers. Breeze kneeled down, and Cressida slid off her back and into the sea of orange flowers. "I bet you need me to make a pile of petals for you," Breeze said.

"Yes, please!" Cressida said.

"I can't wait to see what plan you have

in mind," Breeze said as she pointed her horn up into the sky. "You always have the most creative ideas." Her aquamarine shimmered. Glittery light shot from her horn. And a blue gust of wind swirled and danced through the meadow, sending all the orange petals into the air before they formed a pile at Cressida's feet.

Cressida picked up a clump of petals and rolled it into a ball. Then, she carefully began shaping the petals into a mosquito.

"What is that?" Moon asked, staring at the bug and scrunching up her nose.

"A giant mosquito," Cressida said.

"I don't think we have mosquitoes in the Rainbow Realm," Breeze said.

"I've never even heard of them," Moon said.

"That's lucky!" Cressida said, remembering a time she'd gone on a camping trip with her family and gotten covered in bites. "The real ones aren't any fun to have around. But I'm pretty sure mosquitoes made out of flower petals are harmless."

When Cressida finished sculpting the mosquito, she didn't throw it into the air to make it come alive. Instead, she turned to Breeze and asked, "Could I put this on your back?"

"Sure!" Breeze said.

"Thank you," Cressida said. With the mosquito safely balanced on Breeze's back,

Cressida got to work making seven more. She rested four on Breeze and four on Moon.

"Do you think," Cressida asked after she finished, "that if you both walked very carefully, you could get all the way to the bats without the mosquitoes falling off?"

"Definitely," Breeze said.

Moon nodded in agreement.

"I'll come back and tidy up the petals after the Blast," Breeze said. "I don't want the gust of wind I create to knock over and ruin your mosquitoes."

"Good idea!" Cressida said.

The three slowly made their way under the canopy of elms, across the Meadow of Melodies, through the willow trees, and back to the Monarch Meadow, where they found the gigantic bats still sleeping on the blue kites. Several orange-and-black butterflies perched on the bats, slowly opening and closing their wings.

"Before we wake up the bats, I think we'd better ask the butterflies to leave," Cressida said. "I don't want the bats to accidentally eat them." In school, Cressida had learned that monarch butterflies are poisonous to predators, and that their bright markings were supposed to warn lizards, birds, and frogs to stay away. She figured it wouldn't be good for the butterflies or the bats if the butterflies became an accidental snack.

"I'm glad you thought of that," Breeze said. And then she called out, "Attention! This is Princess Breeze. Monarch butterflies, could you please go to the Meadow of Melodies for a few minutes?"

All at once, the butterflies lifted off the bats and wildflowers and fluttered away.

Cressida looked at Moon. "Could you make the meadow pitch black?"

"Absolutely," Moon said, and took a deep

breath. She pointed her horn toward the enormous, snoring bats. The opal on her ribbon necklace shimmered. Black, glittery light shot out from her horn. And suddenly, the meadow was pitch black.

Within a few seconds, Cressida heard rustling. Then she heard yawning and giant bat wings unfolding and stretching.

"Is it night already?" a squeaky voice asked.

"I could have sworn I just went to bed a few hours ago," another voice squeaked.

"How strange! It feels like the sun just came up," piped a third.

"I guess we'd better look for some food," squeaked a fourth.

Cressida reached for the mosquitoes on

Breeze's back and quickly threw them into the air toward the bats. Then she tossed the mosquitoes on Moon's back in the same direction. In a few seconds, she heard the loud, high-pitched buzzing noise of eight large mosquitoes.

"I hear breakfast!" a voice squeaked, and then she heard the sound of eight giant bats flapping their wings, followed by very loud gulping and chewing noises.

"These are the strangest-tasting mosquitoes I've ever eaten," a voice squeaked.

"I swear they taste like flower petals," squeaked another bat.

"These are tasty! Let's go find some more!"

Soon the sound of flapping bat wings faded into the distance.

"Moon, I think you can make it light again now," Cressida said.

"Sure thing!" Moon said. And suddenly the Monarch Meadow was sunny again.

Cressida blinked and squinted as her eyes adjusted to the brightness. She stared into the distance and spotted the bats, which now, with their wings extended, looked even larger than she had imagined they were. She wished she could tell Corey that she had seen bats that were even bigger than the ones he had told her about. But she knew he would never believe her.

"Do you think they'll be able to find

somewhere to go back to sleep?" Cressida asked.

"Luckily, they're headed straight toward Firefly's domain, the Shimmering Caves," Breeze said. "I'll bet they'll find some-where good to rest there."

The kites slowly stood up, balancing on their tails. They blinked their long, oval eyes and stretched their diamond-shaped bodies. Then, they began to chatter:

"Phew!"

"The bat lying on me smelled terrible!"

"And the one sitting on me was so heavy I couldn't even move my tail!"

"Plus, they snored so loudly!"

All the kites looked at each other and then at Cressida.

"Thank you!" they called out.

"Yes," Breeze said, looking at Cressida and Moon. "I feel so grateful to both of you. I'm very relieved I won't have to cancel the Blast."

"I was glad to help," Cressida said.

"Me too," said Moon. "I'm glad you'll be able to hold the Blast after all. And I'm excited to watch the rest of you fly up into the clouds."

Chapter Eight

A s the kites stretched and jumped, Cressida spotted Flash, Sunbeam, Bloom, Prism, and Firefly trotting toward them.

"We're here and ready to fly!" exclaimed Flash.

"Yes," said Sunbeam. "We can't wait."

"Plus, I'm so hungry I could eat an entire froyanana tree, even the trunk and the leaves," Bloom said. Cressida heard a loud rumbling noise, and the unicorn blushed. "That's my stomach!" Bloom admitted. Cressida giggled.

"I can't wait for the dragon's special feast!" Prism said.

Cressida noticed that Moon was staring at a kite, almost as though she might want to climb onto it. Cressida decided not to say anything, though—she wanted to let Moon make her own decision, at her own pace, and without any pressure.

"Let's go!" Breeze said. "I can already smell the feast."

Cressida inhaled, and sure enough, she could smell food cooking. She looked all around for the dragons and their gigantic vats, but they were nowhere to be seen. "Where are the dragons?" she asked.

"Up in the sky!" Breeze said. "The clouds above this part of the Windy Meadows are special, magic clouds that we can stand and walk and bounce on."

Cressida's eyes widened with excitement. She had always wanted to walk and jump on clouds, but she had never thought that might be possible.

"Well," said Breeze, grinning at her sisters, "are you ready?"

"Yes!" cried Flash, Sunbeam, Bloom, Prism, and Firefly. Moon smiled and said, "I'll be here cheering you on."

While Cressida and Moon watched, the other unicorns raced over to the kites. Each unicorn stepped onto a kite so there were two left—one for Cressida, and one that would have been for Moon.

"Come on, Cressida!" Breeze called out. "Climb onto your kite!"

Cressida turned to Moon to say good-bye, but to her surprise, the unicorn had tears in her eyes. "I'll be right there!" Cressida called out to Breeze. Then she put her arms around Moon's neck. "You look like

you're having a hard time deciding what to do," Cressida said.

Moon nodded. "Now that I'm here look-ing at the kites, I really want to fly in the Blast. Look at how much fun my sisters are already having," she said. "And the dragon's feast is always the best meal I have all year. But I'm still terrified of falling off again. It was just so scary last year."

"I completely understand that," Cressida said. She looked over at the kites and then up at the clouds above them, where she knew the dragons were cooking. She realized she didn't feel so worried about falling off that she couldn't share the cape Ernest had made for her. After all, she wasn't afraid of heights, and she hadn't felt afraid the two other times she had soared through the sky in the Rainbow Realm—first on the boulders in Flash's domain, the Thunder Peaks, and then on the Rainbow Cats in Prism's domain, the Valley of Light.

"Moon," Cressida said, "after you left the front room of the palace this morning, Ernest gave me this special magic cape. It's supposed to keep me safe if I fall off a kite or a cloud. Would you like to share it with me? I don't want to put any pressure on you to get on a kite. But if you'd like to fly in the Blast, I'm sure it's big enough for both of us."

Moon's eyes widened. Relief, and then joy, washed over her face. "Really?" she asked, smiling.

"Really!" Cressida said.

"Are you sure?" Moon asked.

"I'm absolutely, positively sure!" Cressida said.

"I would love that," Moon said. She paused, and furrowed her brow. "But how will we share it?"

"Hmm," Cressida said. "That's a good

question." Even though the cape was roomy enough to fit over both of them, a single kite didn't look like it could safely hold both a girl and a unicorn.

"I can help with that," Breeze said, bounding over. "Just hold up the cape in front of you, and watch this!"

Cressida took off the cape and held it up. It was as wide as one of her bed sheets.

Breeze pointed her horn at the cape. Her aquamarine glittered. Blue, glittery light shot from her horn and a tiny but fierce gust of wind danced above the cape before it plunged downward, ripping the cape in two.

"Voila!" Breeze exclaimed. "Two magic capes!"

"Perfect," Cressida said, laughing. "Thank you, Breeze."

"My pleasure," Breeze said. She reared up with excitement and trotted back to her kite. Cressida draped one sequined cape over Moon's back and tied it around the unicorn's neck.

Then she put on the other one.

"How do I look?" Moon asked, twirling around with excitement.

"Ready to fly!" Cressida responded.

"I'm coming too!" Moon called out, and with her blue sequined cape flapping, she galloped over to her kite and climbed aboard. The other unicorns whinnied and cheered.

Cressida, thrilled her friend felt so much better, sang out, "Here I come!" as she skipped over to the remaining kite.

Chapter Nine

As soon as Cressida stepped onto her giant blue kite, the kite grinned and said, "Pleasure to meet you! My name is Kelly the Kite. We kites drew straws to see who would get to fly with the very first human girl to fly in the Blast. I was the lucky winner!"

"I can't wait," Cressida said. And then,

realizing she felt just a little bit nervous, she added, "I've never ridden a kite before."

"I promise to be extra careful so the ride isn't bumpy," Kelly said. "Just bend your knees a little, hold onto my reins, and you'll be fine." Cressida looked down and saw two sparkling blue strings. She grabbed them, bent her knees, and made sure her feet felt steady.

"Here we go!" Breeze called out. The aquamarine on her ribbon necklace shimmered. Blue, glittery light streamed from her horn. A gentle breeze riffled through Breeze's mane and tail before it blew toward the Meadow of Melodies. Soon Cressida heard "Twinkle, Twinkle, Little Star" playing once again. She smiled at the beauty of the wind chimes' music. Then, as more glittery light shot from Breeze's horn, the strongest gust of wind Cressida had ever felt swirled around Cressida and the unicorn princesses.

Cressida turned to Moon, who looked both excited and scared. "Just remember," Cressida said, "I don't think you'll fall off, but if you do, you're wearing a magic cape."

Kelly and all the other kites lifted off the ground. They formed a line in the air and began to fly in circles, each one higher than the last, as though they were climbing a spiral of wind. She looked down at the Windy Meadows, and then, in the distance, at the other unicorn princesses' domains: Sunbeam's purple Glitter Canyon, Flash's metallic Thunder Peaks, Bloom's green Enchanted Garden, Prism's rainbow-colored Valley of Light, Moon's dark Night Forest, and Firefly's glittery Shimmering Caves. Then she looked at each of the unicorns. All the sisters, including Moon, were grinning from ear to ear. No wonder Breeze and her sisters had been so excited to fly in the Blast.

When they reached the clouds, the kites—with Cressida and the unicorns aboard—flew upward through a long tube made of white fluff. At the end of the tube was an enormous floor made of clouds. They looked, Cressida thought, just like cotton balls. The kites landed, and

Kelly said, "Hop off! And congratulations on taking your first kite ride up to the magic clouds."

Cressida watched as the unicorns leaped off their kites and began jumping on the clouds and giggling. She dropped Kelly's reins and stepped onto the white fluffy floor. It felt soft, like a combination of a bouncy sponge and a cotton ball, under her feet. She jumped and found that she went high up into the air. It was like jumping on the biggest, bounciest mattress she could imagine. "This is so much fun!" she called out.

Breeze bounded over and jumped alongside Cressida. Sunbeam and Flash quickly joined in. And then Bloom, Prism, Moon, and Firefly rushed over, so Cressida and all the princess unicorns were jumping and laughing together.

"I'm so glad I decided to fly after all!" Moon sang out, jumping the highest of all the sisters.

"And I'm glad it was your decision to come with us, and not anyone else's!" Breeze said.

Just then, a voice chortled and then boomed, "The Blast Feast is ready!"

Cressida turned around and saw eight red dragons, all wearing white chef's hats and aprons, stirring gigantic silver vats. She had been so excited by jumping on the clouds that she hadn't even noticed the dragons before.

The same dragon that Cressida had seen carrying vats down to the palace kitchen stepped forward, smiled proudly, and announced, "We've cooked up stewed roinkleberries with creamed froyananas, roasted plums with froyanana sauce, avocado-froyanana soufflé, simmered corn and froyanana chowder, froyanana-oat-bragglenapple bars, froyanana-mango stir-fry, chocolate-eggplant pancakes with diced froyananas, and mushroom-froyanana tarts."

Cressida's stomach turned, and she grimaced at the thought of so many froyananas. Meanwhile, the princess unicorns looked ecstatic.

"Wow!" said Breeze, jumping in backward circles. "You outdid yourselves this year!"

"I can't wait!" Sunbeam exclaimed, dancing with excitement.

"This is the feast of my dreams! So many froyananas!" Bloom sang out.

The dragons laughed, and green flames and blue smoke rose from their nostrils as they emptied the contents of their vats into a row of gold and silver troughs. "Bon appétit!" the dragons called out. The unicorns rushed across the cloud floor and began to gobble down the food in the troughs.

"This stew is incredible!" gushed Moon between bites.

"And the soufflé is amazing," Prism added, licking her lips.

"It's the best chowder I've ever had," Bloom and Sunbeam said in unison.

Cressida smiled as she watched the unicorns eat. She was glad they were enjoying their feast. Just then, a dragon bounced over to her carrying a silver tray piled high with sliced roinkleberries. "Sunbeam

remembered how much you loved these," the dragon said. "All the other dishes have froyananas in them, and Bloom mentioned that, for some strange reason, you don't like those."

"Thank you!" Cressida said. She had first eaten roinkleberries on her first trip to the Rainbow Realm, when she'd visited the Glitter Canyon with Sunbeam, and she knew she loved them.

As Cressida ate the sweet fruit, she realized it was probably about time to go home and fly her own homemade kite up into the clouds above her backyard. She was eager to see Corey, even if she couldn't tell him about her adventures or how he and his book about bats had helped her get the bats off the giant kites. She hoped he still wanted to make a giant bat kite, and she wanted to help him do it.

"You look like you're thinking about going home," Breeze said, looking up from her trough.

"I've had such a wonderful time here," Cressida said, "and I loved the Blast. Thank you so very much for including me. But I do think it's time for me to go home. I'm looking forward to flying kites with my brother."

"You have kites in the human world?" Breeze asked, eyes widening.

"Yes," Cressida said. "In fact, I was making my very first homemade kite this morning when you called me. The only thing I had left to do was make the tail."

"Wow," Breeze said. "Have fun flying it."

Moon took a final bite of the food in her trough and trotted over to Cressida, still wearing her blue, sequined cape. "I heard you say you're about to leave," she said. "Thank you so much for lending me your magic cape. I know I should give it back to you, but," she said, blushing, "I was wondering if I could keep it to wear later on when we all fly back down to the ground."

"Of course," Cressida said, smiling. "I don't need it in the human world. I'm not really a superhero after all."

Then, Flash, Sunbeam, Bloom, Prism, and Firefly joined Cressida, Moon, and Breeze.

"Good bye!" Flash and Sunbeam said.

"Come again soon!" Prism and Bloom said.

"We'll invite you back in no time," Moon said, and Firefly nodded.

Cressida pulled the old-fashioned key with the crystal ball handle from her back pocket. "Take me home, please," she said. The clouds and sky began to spin around her, faster and faster, until they were a swirl of blue and white. Then, everything went pitch black—as dark as Moon had made the Windy Meadows—and Cressida felt the sensation of soaring through the air. She always liked that part of leaving the Rainbow Realm best, but today she especially liked it because it reminded her of flying Kelly the Kite up into the magic clouds.

Soon Cressida felt herself land on the soft forest floor. At first, the trees and sky spun in a blur of green, brown, and blue. Then, the woods slowed to a stop and she found herself sitting beneath the oak tree with the key still in her hands. She stood up, and as she pushed the key into her pocket, she felt something unfamiliar. She pulled it out to discover a long string of the same blue sequins that had been on her magic cape. Attached to the string, a note read,

Here's a magic tail for your kite.
Love, Breeze

Cressida smiled. And then she skipped back toward her house, ready to tie the sequin string to her unicorn kite and fly it in her backyard.

Don't miss our next magical adventure!

Turn the page for a sneak peek . . .

In the top tower of Spiral Palace, Ernest, a wizard-lizard, leafed through a dusty book entitled *Formal Wear for Feathered Friends*. As he turned the pages with his scaly fingers, a bird with messy red feathers and bright green eyes grinned with excitement and hopped from one foot to the other.

Ernest looked up from a page that read,

"Magic Spells for Beginners: Wingtips for Woodpeckers and Spats for Sparrows." He furrowed his green brow and cleared his throat. "Bernadette," he said, "let me make sure I'm getting this right. You want me to turn one of your head feathers into a ball gown?"

"Exactly," Bernadette said. "Last year, I wore an emerald green tuxedo to the Starlight Ball. It matched my eyes perfectly. But this year I want to try a ball gown. I have so many feathers on the top of my head," she continued, looking up at her thick, messy head plumage and grinning sheepishly, "that I was thinking I could spare one to make the perfect dress."

Ernest nodded and flipped to a page

with the words, "Advanced Spells: Turning Feathers and Plumes into Gowns," in large, gold letters across the top. He read for several seconds and asked, "You don't happen to know what a plume is, do you?"

"It's just a fancy word for a feather," Bernadette said, shrugging.

"Then I think I've found just the right spell," Ernest said.

"Fantastic!" Bernadette said, twirling on one talon while she kicked the other foot in the air. "I've been practicing my dance moves all week."

Ernest laughed. "Me too! And I've almost perfected the spell for my tuxedo." He blushed and added, "It just needs a few, um, tweaks." He straightened his pointy hat and pulled his wand from his cloak pocket. "Are you ready for your ball gown?"

"Absolutely!" Bernadette said.

Ernest lifted his wand, pointed it at an unruly feather on Bernadette's head, and chanted, "Feathery Fancily Pleathery Plown! Turn this Ballroom into a Crown!" He stared expectantly at Bernadette. But instead of a gown appearing, thunder rumbled and a giant bolt of gold lightning tore across the sky.

"Oh dear," Ernest said, grimacing. "What did I do wrong this time?"

Emily Bliss lives just down the street from a forest. From her living room window, she can see a big oak tree with a magic keyhole. Like Cressida Jenkins, she knows that unicorns are real.

Sydney Hanson was raised in Minnesota alongside numerous pets and brothers. She has worked for several animation shops, including Nickelodeon and Disney Interactive. In her spare time she enjoys traveling and spending time outside with her adopted brother, a Labrador retriever named Cash. She lives in Los Angeles.

www.sydwiki.tumblr.com